MOUSE AND MOLE
Secret Valentine

BY WONG HERBERT YEE

Green Light Readers
HOUGHTON MIFFLIN HARCOURT
BOSTON NEW YORK

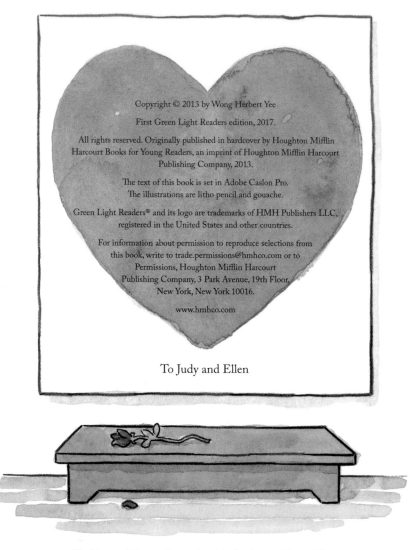

To Judy and Ellen

The Library of Congress has cataloged the hardcover edition as follows:
Yee, Wong Herbert.
Mouse and Mole: secret valentine / Wong Herbert Yee.
p. cm.
A Mouse and Mole story.
Summary: After getting a fluttery feeling while helping Mouse make valentines for each of their friends,
Mole sends her a series of notes and gifts, signing them "your secret valentine."
[1. Best friends—Fiction. 2. Friendship—Fiction. 3. Valentine's Day—Fiction. 4. Mice—
Fiction. 5. Moles (Animals)—Fiction.] I. Title. II. Title: Secret valentine.
PZ7.Y3655Mps 2014
[E]—dc23
2012041660

ISBN: 978-0-547-88719-7 hardcover
ISBN: 978-1-328-74059-5 paperback
ISBN: 978-1-328-97533-1 paper over board

Manufactured in China
SCP 10 9 8 7 6 5 4 3 2 1

4500673255

CONTENTS

Mouse traced a heart on the frosted
windowpane.

"Valentine's Day is coming!"
she squeaked.
Just thinking about it
warmed Mouse
from ear to tail.

"I'd better make a list of our friends,"
she sighed. "Mole is below,
waiting to make valentines."
Mouse nibbled the end of her pencil.

"Let me think . . . there's *Brown Rabbit,*
White Rabbit, and *Squirrel,*" she wrote.
"*Skunk, Porcupine,* and — *Turtle,* too."
Mouse twirled her tail.
"It seems I'm forgetting someone?"

"Silly me!" she giggled.

"I left out my best friend!"

Mouse added *Mole* to the list.

She drew a heart next to his name.

Mouse got a funny
feeling inside —
like butterflies
in her stomach.

Downstairs, Mole was getting ready
to make valentines.
Mole rubbed his snout.
"Let me see . . .
We will need
paper and pencils,
scissors and glue."

Mole laid everything out on the table.

"Valentine's Day is about *love*," he sighed.
Mole felt his face flush.
He was thinking about his
neighbor upstairs, Mouse.
Mole got a funny
feeling inside —
like butterflies
in his stomach. TAP-TAP-TAP.
A knock on the door made Mole jump.
"Come in, Mouse," he said.
"I have been waiting."

Mouse stepped into Mole's hole.

"Are you feeling okay?" she asked.

"You look a bit flushed."

Mole's cheeks turned redder still.

"I was busy fetching stuff

to make valentines," he explained.

"So, what's the plan?" Mouse wondered.

Mole took a piece of pink paper

and folded it in half.

He drew a curvy line in pencil.

"That looks like my tail," giggled Mouse.

"Do not be silly!" chuckled Mole.

He cut along the line with scissors.

Snip, snip, snip!

"Presto!" Mole unfolded the paper.

"Why, it's a *heart!*" Mouse exclaimed.

"You are *too* clever, Mole!"

Mole laid the pink sheet on a red one.

"Pencil the message *here*," he said.

Mole cut out more heart shapes.

Mouse thought of things to say.

She nibbled the end of her pencil.

On one card

Mouse wrote:

BE MINE.

On another she put:

TOO COOL!

"How many do we need?" Mole asked.

Mouse peeked at her list. "Six will do."

"A half dozen it is!" agreed Mole.

Mouse squinted at the red paper.

"These pencil lines are hard to read."

Mole handed Mouse a tube of glue.

"Trace them over with this, Mouse.

I will be right back."

Mole returned with a jar of silver glitter.

He sprinkled it all over the red sheet.

Mole tipped the paper up and gave it a
TAP-TAP-TAP. The glitter that didn't
stick to the letters slid off.

Mouse clapped her paws in delight.
"You are not only *clever*, Mole,
but *artistic* as well!"
Mole blushed
a valentine red.

Mole found a card under his door.

It was a valentine from Mouse.

Mole got that feeling inside again —

like butterflies in his stomach.

He hid the card

in a drawer.

Mole knocked on Mouse's door:

TAP-TAP-TAP.

"Hello, Mole!"
said Mouse.

"Hello, Mouse!"
said Mole.

"Ready to deliver our valentines?"

"I am ready and waiting," said Mouse.

"Let's start with Turtle."

Together, they took the
path to the pond.

"B-r-r!" Mole shivered.

"I forgot my hat.

You go ahead, Mouse.

I will catch up."

When Mole hurried back down the path,

he saw his friend hiding behind a fir tree.

"Hey, Mouse!" he called.

"Quiet," she shushed.

"Turtle is just

leaving now."

Together, they waited . . . and waited.

Mole peeked from behind the trunk.

"The coast is clear," he waved.

Mouse slid the card under Turtle's door.

"Rabbits' place is next," she said.

After that, they visited Skunk,

and then Porcupine.

There was only one valentine left.

Mole gazed up the trunk of the elm.

"Squirrel is *nuts* to live

up there!" he gasped.

Mouse handed Mole

the last card.

"Your turn!" she gulped.

Mole looked at Mouse.

Mouse looked at Mole.

"Mailbox?" Mole pointed.

"Mailbox!" Mouse nodded.

Together, they headed back to the oak.

Mole went down in his hole.

"Shall we meet later for lunch?"

Mouse went up to her house.

"Lunch later!" she agreed.

Mouse found a card under *her* door:
She got that feeling
inside again —
like butterflies
in her stomach.

♥ ♥ ♥

Mole saw Mouse coming down the street.
Mouse had a goofy grin on her face.
BUMP! she walked *smack* into a lamppost.

"Mouse, are you okay?" Mole cried.
Mouse felt her face flush.
"I was thinking about what to order,"
she explained. Really, Mouse was
daydreaming about her *secret valentine*.

The diner was packed. Luckily, there was an empty booth in back.

Mouse shivered. "I need something hot."
She ordered **Cheddar Cheese Soup.**
Mole had worms, as usual.
"Oops! I forgot to say *lightly fried.*"
Mole went to
remind the cook.

Mouse read the poster above Mole's seat.

The waiter returned with their orders.

Mole dug into his bowl of worms.

Mouse sipped her soup.

I wonder if Mole noticed the poster?

The waiter came back with another dish.

He set it in front of Mouse.

"Someone is hungry!" munched Mole.

Mouse stared at the block of cheese.

It was cut in the shape of a heart.

There was a message carved on top:

BE MY
CINDERELLA?
FROM YOUR
MOZZAFELLA
XOXO

Mouse blushed a valentine red.

She looked around the diner.

My secret valentine is clever! thought Mouse.

Mole was too busy

eating to notice.

Mouse was going on a secret mission.

She planned to find out *who*

her secret valentine was.

She checked the card

for clues.

Mouse twirled her tail.

"NUTS?—Squirrel is *crazy* for nuts . . .

Perhaps he is *nuts* about me?"

Down the steps

Mouse crept.

Mole was on a secret mission too.

He waited until Mouse left.

Up the steps he crept. Mole took

the back way into town.

When no one was looking, he slipped

into **The Sweet Shop.**

Boxes of candy filled the rack.

Mole rubbed his snout.

He picked out a heart-shaped box.

Mole set it on the counter.

"Sweets for your sweet?" asked the cashier
with a wink. Mole felt his face flush.
Ka-ching! rang
the register.
He grabbed the
box of chocolates
and hurried outside.

Mole ducked into the flower shop
next door. Inside were
all kinds of flowers in
a rainbow of colors.
Mole tapped his foot.
"*Red*, I should think."
"Roses are *my* favorite too,"
whispered the clerk in his ear.
Mole nearly knocked a pot off the shelf.
"S-s-six will do," he stammered.
The clerk nodded. "A half dozen it is!"
Ka-ching! rang
the register.

Back to the oak Mole scurried.

"Yikes!" Mole dove behind a bush.

Mouse was up ahead,

spying on Porcupine.

"Perhaps Porcupine is *stuck*

on me?" Mouse giggled

to herself.

Mole waited until the coast was clear.

He dumped the candy on the table.

Mole picked a flower from the bunch
and set it aside.

He pulled the petals off the others,
one by one. *"She loves me —*
she loves me not . . ."

Soon there was only one petal left.
Mole plucked it off the stem.
"She loves me!" he sighed.

Mole got a funny feeling inside —

like butterflies in his stomach.

He wrote a message inside the box.

Sweets for my Sweet!
Meet me at four
On the dance floor
Your Secret
Valentine
xoxo

Mole covered it with rose petals

and put the chocolates on top.

"Sweets for my sweet!" he chuckled.

Mouse trudged back to the oak.

She had not discovered her secret valentine.

"Squirrel is *nuts* about Chipmunk,"

muttered Mouse to herself.

"And Porcupine is *stuck* on Hedgehog."

Skunk was not sweet on her either.

Mouse spotted the box on her stoop.

"Eek!" she squeaked.

"My secret valentine

has struck again!"

Mouse sniffed
the rose petals.
"How lovely!"
she sighed.

Mouse popped
a chocolate
into her mouth.

"My secret valentine is not only *clever*,"
she munched, "but *artistic,* too!"
Mouse did not find a card inside.
She had hoped for an invitation
to the dance by now.

"Today is the party," murmured Mouse.
"Perhaps Mole didn't see the poster —
But what about my *secret* valentine?"
Mouse paced to and fro.

Every time she passed the box of candy,
she ate another. *"He loves me,"*
munched Mouse.
"He loves me not . . ."

Soon there was only one chocolate left.

Mouse gobbled it up.

"He loves me!" she declared.

Mouse tipped the box up,

looking for more.

The petals slid down

onto the table.

Mouse saw the message on the bottom:

Sweets for my Sweet!
Meet me at four
On the dance floor.
Your Secret
Valentine
xoxo

Mouse glanced at the clock.

"Mercy me!" she squeaked.

"It's nearly four now!"

Mouse rummaged through her closet.

"*Red*, I should think."

Quickly, she pulled on the dress.

♥ ♥ ♥

The Valentine's party was in full swing!

The jug band played a snappy tune.

Everyone was dancing with a partner.

Everyone but Mole, that is.

He sat on the bench by himself.

Mole glanced at the clock.

It was already past four.

"Ratty-rat-rat!" he muttered.

Mole rubbed his snout.

"Perhaps Mouse does not like dancing?"

He plucked a petal off the rose.

The one he had saved for Mouse.

"She loves me . . ."

Mole plucked another.

"She loves me — not!"

Whoosh! a sudden gust
of wind blew the petals
from his paw.

Mouse yanked the door shut. She checked her coat and hat. "I hope I'm not too late!" she huffed.

Mole noticed a commotion in the room.

Someone was crossing the dance floor.

The jug band
stopped playing.

The crowd parted to make way . . .

Plop! Mole toppled right off the bench.

Mole spotted Mouse!

Mouse spotted Mole!

Mouse twirled her tail.

My secret valentine

is clever, she thought.

Mouse tapped her foot.

My secret valentine

is artistic, too . . .

Suddenly, Mouse pictured acorns.

"NUTS!" she squeaked.

"Mole is crazy about acorns!"

Mouse dashed across the room.

"Why . . . my *secret valentine* is . . .

YOU!" she cried.

Mole's cheeks turned rose red.

He handed Mouse the flower.

Two of its petals were missing.

"Happy Valentine's Day!" murmured Mole.

Mouse got a funny feeling inside —

like butterflies in her stomach.

"Happy Valentine's Day to you, too!"

Mouse blushed.

Mole chuckled. "I was beginning to think you did not like to dance."

"Do not be silly!" Mouse giggled.

She took Mole's left paw in her right.

Mole took Mouse's right paw in his left.

Together, they stepped out onto the dance floor.

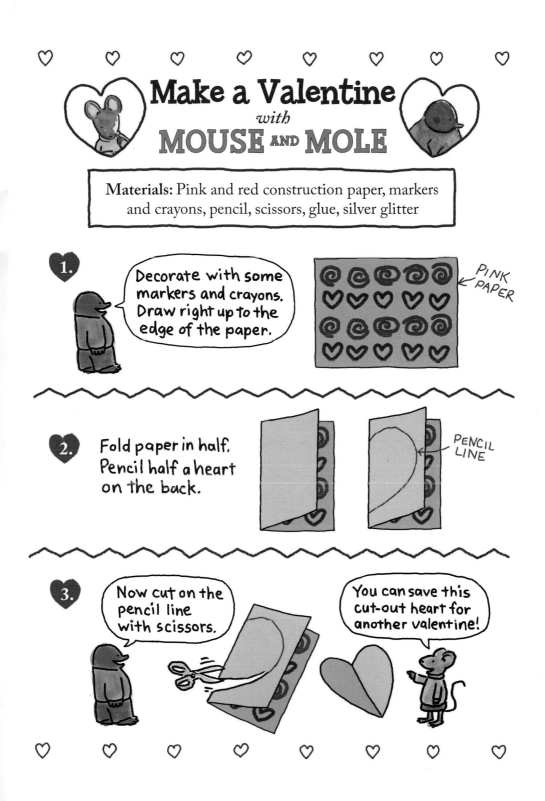

Make a Valentine
with
MOUSE AND MOLE

Materials: Pink and red construction paper, markers and crayons, pencil, scissors, glue, silver glitter

1. Decorate with some markers and crayons. Draw right up to the edge of the paper.

PINK PAPER

2. Fold paper in half. Pencil half a heart on the back.

PENCIL LINE

3. Now cut on the pencil line with scissors.

You can save this cut-out heart for another valentine!